A novelization by Francine Hughes
Based on the screenplay written by
Leo Benvenuti & Steve Rudnick and Timothy Harris & Herschel Weingrod

SCHOLASTIC INC.
New York Toronto London Auckland Sydney

ISBN 0-590-94555-6

12 11 10 9 8 7 6 5 4 3 2 1   6 7 8 9/9 0 1/0

Printed in the U.S.A.   40

First Scholastic printing, November 1996

1

1973

Stars twinkled brightly. A full moon lit a quiet, tree-lined street.

Thump, thump, thump. A loud noise broke the silence. A ten-year-old boy dribbled a basketball. Up and down he went. Down and up the driveway of his house. He shot the ball at the basket. Then *thump, thump, thump*, he shot again. He wouldn't give up. He wanted each move to be perfect.

The stars, the moonlight, the basket,

and the ball: It all seemed magical. And the boy — Michael Jordan — could play forever.

The porch light switched on suddenly. Michael blinked. His dad stood on the steps.

"Michael?" Mr. Jordan called softly. "What are you doing out here, son? It's after midnight."

Michael dribbled. He had to keep the ball moving. "I couldn't sleep, Pop," he explained.

His father smiled. "Neither can we with all this noise. Come on. Let's go inside."

"Just one more shot?" Michael pleaded.

Mr. Jordan looked at Michael's eager face. "All right. Just one."

Michael took aim. *Swish!* The ball sailed through the hoop. A perfect shot.

"All right," his father said. "Shoot it again."

Swish!

"Getting pretty good, son," Mr. Jordan told Michael. He tossed him the ball. "Go ahead. Shoot till you miss."

Michael took shot after shot. "Hey," he said as he let them fly. "Do you think I can be really good? Good enough to get into college?"

"If you get really good," his father told him, "you can do anything you want to, Michael."

"I want to play at North Carolina," Michael said. "On a championship college team. Then I want to play in the NBA. And once I've done all that? I want to play baseball, just like you, Dad."

Mr. Jordan chuckled. "Baseball. Now that's a sport. And when you're finished with that? I suppose you are going to *fly,* huh?"

Fly? Could he fly? Michael wondered. He gripped the ball tight. He drove toward the basket. Smooth. Easy. Michael leaped into the air. Higher . . . higher. He soared. Just the way he would . . .

. . . in 1982
at North Carolina on a championship
team
. . . in 1984 and 1992
at the Olympics
. . . in 1985
as NBA rookie of the year
. . . and year after year,
leading the Chicago Bulls to victory.

Michael was the best. A star. A legend.
Now what? he wondered one day. *What
else can I do?* Then he remembered that
conversation with his father. And he knew
the answer.
Baseball!

2

Michael Jordan playing *baseball*? Michael Jordan quitting *basketball*?

Newspapers screamed the headlines. TV bulletins hit the air. Shock waves traveled the world. No one could believe it. Everyone talked about it. But zillions of miles away in outer space, no one cared.

Past the moon, the planets, and faraway galaxies . . . on a bright bright star . . . stood Moron Mountain Theme Park. And there on Moron Mountain, no one knew

Michael at all.

The outer-space park had merry-go-rounds, roller coasters, and fiery meteor rides. Still, it hardly had any business.

And Swackhammer, the big boss of Moron Mountain, was angry.

Swackhammer paced back and forth in his office. He had green skin, a big round body, and an ugly purple suit. His pointy ears quivered as he watched the video monitors.

"We need new attractions!" he told his Nerdluck workers.

The five Nerdlucks looked at each other. They were weak, tiny creatures, all the colors of the rainbow. They twisted their bow ties and sighed. They had to agree with Swackhammer. It went with the job.

"New attractions!" they shouted back. "Right!"

"Something nutty," Swackhammer went on.

"Nutty!" agreed Bang and Blanko.

"Wacky!" cried Bupkus.

"Looney!" shouted the smallest Nerd-luck, Nawt.

"Did you say LOONEY?" Pound, the Nerdluck leader, sat by the computer. He typed in "Looney." A big bold Bugs Bunny cartoon played on-screen. Looney Tunes music filled the room.

"Yes, looney!" exclaimed Swackhammer. He jumped to his feet. "That's it! Bring me the Looney Tunes!"

"Sir!" said Nawt. "Just noticing, sir. The Looney Tunes are from Earth. What if they can't come?"

Swackhammer pounded his big beefy fist. "Make 'em!" he ordered.

3

Back on Earth, Michael Jordan strode up to bat. He was in the minor leagues now. And the stadium was packed.

Every seat was filled. Every eye zeroed in on Michael. Michael Jordan playing baseball! That's why they had come.

A fastball whistled past the plate.

"Strike one!" called the umpire.

Cameras flashed. Reporters scribbled.

Michael sighed. He was really just learning to play. Why did everyone have to make a fuss?

Another pitch whizzed by. Strike two.

The catcher wanted to help. After all, this was Michael Jordan standing in front of him. *The* Michael Jordan — even if he was on the other team. He signaled the pitcher.

"Next one's a curveball," he whispered to Michael. "Don't swing."

"What?" said Michael. He was too surprised to move as the ball curved over the plate.

"Ball!" yelled the ump. The catcher winked at Michael. Then he signaled the pitcher again. "Here's another one," he told Michael. "Slider. Don't swing."

But the pitch looked good. Michael swung.

"Strike three!" called the ump.

The catcher shrugged. "Nice talking to you," he told Michael.

Michael trudged back to the dugout. His teammates slapped him on the back. They said, "Good try." Michael knew they were being nice. But he wished he could be treated like everyone else.

"Hey, Podolak. Come here," the manager called to a guy on the sidelines. "I want you to make sure no one bothers Michael. I want him to be the happiest player in the world. Make sure Michael's the happiest player in the world."

Pudgy and awkward, Stan Podolak hurried to the dugout. "Mr. Jordan?" he began.

All at once, a loud booming noise filled the air. A spaceship plunged from the sky. Then it disappeared from sight.

Michael blinked. Did he really see that ship? And did it really say Moron Mountain on it?

4

Inside the spaceship, the Nerdlucks tumbled about. "Hang on!" cried Pound. "Hanging on!" the Nerdlucks called back.

Pound flipped a switch. The ship drilled into the ground, nose first.

Down, down, down they went. They dove through dirt and rocks. Past layer after layer of earth. Then something loomed ahead: a big bull's-eye with a WB on it. Warner Bros.!

Pound grinned. They were right on target for Looney Tune Land.

The Nerdlucks burst through the WB. Cartoon mountains, lakes, and trees met their eyes. They had arrived!

Meanwhile, Looney Tune life went on as normal. Bugs Bunny chomped on a carrot and raced down a road.

"Come back here, you silly wabbit!" Elmer Fudd called after him.

The ship hovered just above Bugs. The door slid open. Bugs eyed the little Nerdlucks up and down. "I'll be with you in a second, folks," he told them. "After I finish with nature boy here."

Elmer stepped in front of Bugs. He was so happy to catch up, he didn't see the ship. "All wight, you pesky wabbit," he said. "I've got you now!"

Wham! The ship's ramp lowered right on Elmer. The aliens scurried down. "One small step for *moi*," Pound declared.

"One giant leap for Moron Mountain!" exclaimed Bang.

"And one giant headache for Elmer Fudd," Bugs said.

Bang gazed up at Bugs. "We seek the one they call Bugs Bunny."

"Is he around?" asked Blanko.

Bugs scratched his head, pretending to think. "Hmmm. Does he have long ears like these?" He wiggled his ears.

"Yeah!" shouted the Nerdlucks.

"And does he hop around?" Bugs jumped from side to side. "Like this?"

"Yeah!" shouted the Nerdlucks.

"And does he say, 'What's up, Doc?' like this? . . . 'Eh, what's up, Doc?'"

"Yeah!" said the excited Nerdlucks.

Bugs shook his head. "Nope. Never heard of him."

"Aww," said Nawt, disappointed.

Bugs walked away, grinning. Who said there was intelligent life in outer space?

But Bugs didn't get far. Five giant ray guns pointed right at him.

"Okay, bunny," Pound ordered. "Gather up your Tune pals. We're taking you for a ride!"

5

At that very moment, Michael Jordan sat in Stan Podolak's car. Stan was driving Michael home, doing his best to make him happy. But they'd gotten lost again and again. Finally Stan pulled up to Michael's house. His old car sputtered and jerked. Michael felt glad to be home.

"Thanks for the ride, Sherm," Michael said. He tried to get out. But the door was jammed.

"It's *Stan*, Mike," Stan said, gazing up at his hero. "But you can call me Sherm if you want. Because I've followed your whole career. And I just think . . ."

"Man, stop that!" Michael interrupted. "How do you get out of here? The door doesn't work."

Stan nodded. But he didn't really hear. "This is a nice house. Do you need anything done to it? A little painting? A little plastering? I'd be happy to . . ."

"Stan!" Michael said again. "How do I get out of this car?"

Stan reached over and shoved the door. It sprang open — but only a few inches.

Michael squeezed himself out. Then he looked at Stan. The poor guy seemed so sad, so upset he couldn't do anything.

"I appreciate it," Michael told him. "Thanks."

Stan beamed. He waved happily and the broken-down car took off in a cloud of smoke. *There,* Michael thought. *That's better.* He turned to go inside. But he stopped in his tracks. A giant bulldog was bounding over.

"Come on, Charles," Michael begged. "No! Not today . . ."

Too late. Charles knocked Michael to the ground. He licked his face and slobbered all over him.

Michael struggled to his feet. "Come on, Charles," he ordered as a van pulled up. Michael's wife, Juanita, drove.

A Little League team spilled out the back door and Juanita chased Charles away.

Michael smiled as his nine-year-old son trudged past.

"Hey, Jeff," he called. "You okay? How was your game?"

Jeff kept his head down and his eyes on the ground. "I don't want to talk about it," he muttered.

"Daddy, Daddy!" shouted six-year-old Marcus. Then four-year-old Jasmine jumped into his arms. Michael hugged them both. He kissed Juanita hello. But his mind was still on Jeff. What was wrong?

"Well, he went two for five. And he lost thirty-two points in his batting average," Juanita explained.

"Better than me," Michael told her.

Inside, Jeff, Marcus, and Jasmine watched TV. Michael was on the sports news, striking out.

Michael didn't want to see that — again. So he quickly changed the channel.

Road Runner came on-screen, running across the desert. "Beep-beep!"

Smiling happily, the Jordan family sat back to watch. But Porky Pig interrupted the show.

"Stop the cartoon!" he cried. "We've got an em-em-m-m — an emergency meeting of cartoon characters to go to!"

Road Runner zipped away. Porky trailed behind. And the screen went blank.

6

Emergency meeting! Every Looney Tune character scurried to Town Hall. Porky Pig, Road Runner, Yosemite Sam, Sylvester and Tweety, Foghorn Leghorn, and the others filed into seats.

Onstage, Bugs and Elmer Fudd stood wrapped in chains. The Nerdlucks paced around them.

Town Hall grew quiet as Daffy Duck strode up the aisle. He headed straight for the stage. "So what's the big emergency?" he demanded.

Pound took the microphone. "You are all our prisoners!" he announced.

These tiny aliens? Capturing *them*? Town Hall rocked with laughter. Daffy sputtered. Foghorn Leghorn clucked. Yosemite Sam slapped his knee.

Tiny Nawt grabbed the mike. It was three times his size. "We are taking you to our theme park in outer space," he ordered. "You will be our slaves there."

What could these little guys do? Daffy Duck clutched his chest in pretend fear. But Yosemite Sam took the challenge. He leaped onstage. "We ain't a-goin' nowheres!" he shouted.

Yosemite lifted his gun. Pound lifted his. The guns stood barrel to barrel. *Boom!* Yosemite gazed down.

"Aaagh!" he cried. Pound had shrunk him to the size of a chihuahua.

The Nerdlucks turned their ray guns to the audience. Daffy raised his arms.

"Let's get them aboard the ship!" yelled Pound.

"Eh, not so fast, Doc." Bugs finally spoke up. "You have to give us a chance. We've got to defend ourselves."

Pound waved his gun. "Says who?"

Quickly Bugs slipped out of his chains. Then he scribbled in a notebook. A moment later he showed the book to Pound. "Read 'em and weep, boys."

"Hmmm," said Pound. " 'Rules for Capturing Cartoon Characters.' "

Nawt read over Pound's shoulder. " 'Give them a chance to defend themselves.' "

The Nerdlucks had to agree. After all, it was in the rules. So the Looney Tunes called a conference.

Commander-in-chief Bugs pulled down a war map. Then he straightened his uniform and tapped his pointer.

"The way I see it . . ." Bugs began.

"Uh! Uh! I got it!" cried Porky. "We ch-ch-challenge them to a spelling b-b-bee."

Elmer rattled his chains. "A bowling tournament!"

"Sufferin' succotash!" said Sylvester. "I say we get a ladder. We wait till the old lady's outta the room. Then we grab that little bird!"

The meeting was going downhill. Fast. Bugs rapped his pointer on the table. Then he pointed to a picture of the Nerdlucks.

"Now, uh, what are we looking at here?" he asked. "A small race of invading aliens."

"Small arms," Daffy said. "Short legs."

"Not vewy fast," said Elmer.

"Can't jump high," Porky added.

"Uh-huhh . . ." they all said.

Bugs smiled slowly. He had an idea. Daffy grinned, too. He had the same exact thought. Then it dawned on them all — even Elmer.

"We challenge you to a basketball game!" Bugs told Pound a minute later.

"Basketball it is!" said Pound.

"All right! Basketball!" cried Bang and Bupkus, Blanko, and Nawt.

Then Bupkus scratched his head. "What *is* basketball?"

In a flash, Daffy lowered the lights and turned on a film projector. An old movie came on-screen. Five tall, skinny guys were shooting baskets — and missing. They could barely pass the ball.

"And now," said the narrator, "here is how it's done in the NBA." The Nerdlucks nodded and watched. "The NBA features the best players in the world . . ."

"The best players in the world," Nawt said dreamily.

"The world . . ." Bupkus echoed.

"Hmm . . ." the Nerdlucks all said at once.

They knew what they had to do.

7

The Nerdlucks didn't know much about the NBA. But they had Swackhammer to answer to. And they knew they had to do everything they could to win. So they headed to New York, to watch a game.

Bupkus stood on Pound's shoulders. Nawt stood on Bupkus's shoulders. They covered themselves with a hat and raincoat. Then they wobbled into Madison Square Garden.

"Excuse me," Nawt said as they bumped into fans. "Pardon."

Finally they plopped into a seat.

A woman sat in the next seat. She leaned away from the aliens and nudged her husband. "This guy is weird," she hissed.

"Would you let me watch the game?" the man pleaded. "Charles Barkley is killing the Knicks!"

"Hey!" Pound whispered. "Someone is killing someone!"

They watched Charles slam-dunk the ball. Bupkus nodded happily. "He's mine!" he told the others.

Bupkus melted into a puddle of purple slime. The woman held her nose and lifted her feet. The slime turned to mist. Then it drifted over to Charles. *Sssst!* It slid into his ear.

Charles twitched. He shook. His legs jerked every which way. *Ssst!* The mist slid out his other ear. It floated back to Pound and Nawt, and back under the raincoat.

A second later, Bupkus peeked out. He

held a container filled with purple smoke. "I got him!" he said. "I got his talent!"

Meanwhile, the coach and all the Suns crowded around Charles. "Go get the doctor!" the coach ordered.

"But I'm fine," Charles insisted.

But he couldn't catch or dribble. He couldn't even high-five a teammate.

Charles couldn't do anything at all.

Next the Nerdlucks zeroed in on the Knicks. An instant later, Patrick Ewing jerked and twitched just like Charles. Then he tripped over his feet, sliding across the floor.

"Got him!" crowed Pound. He held up a glass of purple smoke and grinned.

The Nerdlucks struck Larry Johnson and Muggsy Bogues of the Charlotte Hornets. Then they hit Shawn Bradley of the 76ers, the tallest man in the NBA. And afterward, not one of those players could play.

8

In Looney Tune Land, everyone gathered at the basketball court.

Bugs called them all into a circle. "Okay," he said. "Has anyone played basketball before?"

No one said a word. Then Daffy burst on court. "I have, Coach!" he shouted. "And there's an important question I need to ask."

Daffy spun on his heel and modeled his fancy uniform. "What do you think?" he asked. "Does this go with my feathers?"

Before anyone could answer, the Nerd-lucks arrived. They wanted practice time, too.

Bugs shrugged. "Let the pip-squeaks knock themselves out!"

Pound bounced a ball. He could barely hold onto it.

"Too bad you can't practice getting taller, boys," Daffy laughed.

The Nerdlucks formed a circle. They each held a bottle of purple smoke. They clinked glasses, then downed the swirling mist. One loud burp rang out. Smiling, they placed their tiny hands on the basketball.

The ball began to glow. Brighter . . . brighter . . . and brighter still. Bit by bit, the Nerdlucks' feet pumped up. Then their legs grew longer . . . their arms wider. Muscles popped out everywhere. The faces of the NBA players seemed to hang in the air. Then they changed . . . changed into entirely different faces.

Evil ones.

The Nerdlucks stood transformed. They towered over Bugs and the others, tall as trees. Their sighs turned into roars. Their hands became fists. A strange new light blazed in their eyes.

Pound picked up the ball. The Looney Tune characters gasped. The basketball looked small as a baseball now. Pound twirled it, then tossed it. It flew right through the hoop.

Daffy's jaw dropped open. "Those little pip-squeaks?" he sputtered. "They turned into superstars."

"Sufferin' succotash," cried Sylvester. "They're Mon*stars*!"

Bugs chomped on a carrot. "I think we need a little bit of help."

9

That afternoon, Michael was playing golf with his friend Larry Bird. Stan buzzed around them, eager to help. He checked Michael's clubs. He polished his golf balls.

Michael always liked to win when he played Larry. It went back to their days as professional basketball players — playing on different teams.

Larry stepped up to the tee. He practiced his swing.

"Mike," he said, "the NBA has to face the truth. These players are in bad shape.

The NBA needs new players now. New players with talent."

Michael sighed. Sure, the NBA was in trouble. But Michael was worried about his NBA friends. Would they ever be okay?

Larry swung. The ball soared high in the air.

"Nice shot," Stan said before the ball hit the ground. "Very nice."

It was Michael's turn next. Stan handed him a club. Then Michael set his ball on the tee. He gazed up the fairway to the hole. He didn't see Bugs pop out of the ground. Nobody did. Quick, before anyone noticed, Bugs switched balls.

Once again Michael faced the tee. He lifted his club. *Crack!* Michael hit Bugs's special ball.

The ball swooped up to the clouds. It flew long and straight. Then it landed right near Larry's. Larry smiled. He hated to lose to Michael.

But as they drove up in the cart,

On a distant planet in outer space, Swackhammer needs a new attraction at his intergalactic amusement park. "Bring me those Looney Tunes!" he demands.

The alien Nerdlucks carry out Swackhammer's orders. "Okay, Bunny," Pound says. "Gather up your Tune pals. We're taking you for a ride!"

Bugs Bunny sizes up the competition.

The Looney Tunes get a chance to defend themselves. "We challenge you to a basketball game," says Bugs.

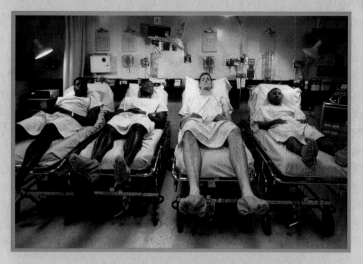

The Nerdlucks don't know a *thing* about basketball, so they steal the talent from Patrick Ewing, Larry Johnson, Shawn Bradley, and Muggsy Bogues, landing the players in the hospital.

Suddenly, the Looney Tunes aren't so sure of victory — because those tiny Nerdlucks have turned into huge MONSTARS!

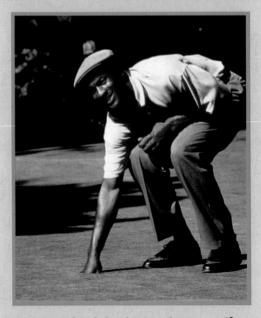

The Looney Tunes need help . . . they need talent . . .
they need Michael Jordan, basketball superstar!

One minute Michael Jordan is playing golf . . .
and the next he's on his way to Looney Tune Land!

Bugs lets Michael know just how badly the Tunes
need his help!

Michael Jordan decides he's not going to take those
aliens lying down. "Let's play some basketball!"
he says.

At a Tune Squad practice session, Yosemite Sam "shoots" the ball . . .

. . . and Daffy gets slam-ducked.

The members of the Tune Squad are ready for the big game . . . or are they?

After a bad first half, Bugs Bunny comes up with a secret formula to save the Tunes . . . and maybe even the world!

Michael Jordan sets out to put the Monstars in their place.

With only ten seconds to go, Michael Jordan scores
the winning basket. Now Bugs and his pals can go
back to their looney life on the planet Earth.

Michael's ball began to move. It zigged. It zagged. It rolled closer to the hole, then closer still.

The ball had a piece of metal inside. And Bugs was burrowing underground, holding a magnet!

Michael and Larry leaped off the cart. They followed the crazy ball.

"It's impossible!" cried Larry.

The two friends watched in amazement. The ball twisted and turned until . . . *thwack!* It dropped in the hole.

"Nothing but the bottom of the cup," Michael crowed.

Stan whipped out his camera. "Now reach for the ball," he directed Michael. "And smile!"

Michael grinned as he bent over. He fumbled around in the cup. What was going on? The ball wasn't there! But wait! Something *was* there. Something was grabbing his hand. Pulling him down!

Just as Stan took the shot, Michael disappeared down the hole.

10

Down, down, down. Michael felt himself tugged underground. Through tunnels, passageways, and caves . . . right through the WB bull's-eye. Finally he landed in Looney Tune Land with a thump.

Bugs gazed down at him. "Look out for that first step, Doc," he said. "It's a lulu."

A cartoon? Talking to him? Michael shook his head to clear it. But nothing changed. Bugs was still there.

"Bugs Bunny?" Michael whispered.

"You were expecting maybe the Easter Bunny?" Bugs asked.

"You're a cartoon," Michael said, amazed. "You're not real."

"Not real, eh?" said Bugs. "Then how could I do this?" And he planted a big kiss on Michael's cheek.

Just then the other Looney Tunes hurried over.

"It's Michael!" they cried. "It's Michael Jordan!"

"I tawt I saw a Michael Jordan!" chirped Tweety. "And I did!"

"Pardon me, Mr. Jordan," Porky Pig said. "Can I have your auto-autog-g-g-autog-g-g — John Hancock?"

"Back off!" Daffy pushed his way through. He wore a white smock and carried a stethoscope. "Let the duck-tor take a look."

He pulled Michael into a swivel chair. Then he jacked it up. *Whoosh!* Michael shot up like a rocket.

"Oops," Daffy said. "A little high." He pulled a lever. "Going down!" Michael plummeted.

"Now how about a spin?" Daffy asked.

"No!" Michael shouted. But around and around he whirled. Finally Daffy reached out with his little finger and stopped the chair.

"Say 'ah'!" said Daffy. He stuck a thermometer into Michael's mouth.

"Agh!" Michael choked. The thermometer turned red.

And redder.

And redder.

Kaboom! It exploded.

"All right!" Daffy exclaimed. And he stamped Michael's head *A-OK*.

When Michael caught his breath, he finally spoke. "What's going on here?"

Bugs jumped into Michael's lap. "Why Michael," he said, "I thought you'd never ask."

Speaking quickly, Bugs told Michael everything. "Little aliens . . . theme park

. . . slaves . . . basketball game . . . big huge aliens . . . WE NEED YOUR HELP!"

Michael shook his head. "But I'm a baseball player now," he protested.

And he kept protesting . . . all the way to the gym.

11

At the Looney Tune gym, Michael said, "Look. I want to help. But I haven't played basketball in a long time. My timing is all off."

Bugs waved his paw around the room. "We'll fix your timing. Look at this place!"

Michael looked.

"We got hoops!" Daffy declared.

The basketball hoops were rusty and bent.

"We got weights!" Elmer said proudly.

In the corner of the room, cobwebs hung from the barbells.

"We got balls!" said Sylvester. He opened a locker and dozens of balls tumbled out. Sylvester sputtered, buried under the pile.

Michael shook his head. "This place is a mess."

"Mess?" Daffy opened his eyes wide. "You worried about a little mess? A little spit shine will fix everything. Spit shine!" he shouted.

"Spit shine!" everyone echoed, spitting on the floor.

Taz whirled in, mopping in circles. "Lemony fresh!" he told Michael.

"You guys are nuts!" Michael exclaimed.

"Correction!" Bugs told him. "We're Looney Tunes!"

That did it. Michael had to laugh, right along with Bugs and the others.

But the laughter died quickly. The Monstars burst into the gym.

Pound raised a giant fist. "We're the Mean Team."

Pound gazed at Michael and sneered. "Let's see what you've got, chump."

Chump? thought Michael. *Who's he calling chump?* But Michael wouldn't let these guys get to him. He was a baseball player now.

"I don't play basketball anymore," he told them.

Bang grinned a big evil grin. "Maybe you're chicken." He flapped his arms like wings. "*Buck-buck-buck.* Chicken!"

"I say," put in Foghorn, patting his feathers. "I resemble that remark."

Quickly, Pound reached for Michael. He palmed him and the basketball together. An instant later, he slam-dunked Michael into the basket.

Michael bounced once. Twice. Then he shook himself back into his normal shape.

"Look at your hero now!" Pound shouted.

Michael narrowed his eyes. "You guys

are making a big mistake," he warned.

"Yeah?" said Bang. "And you're all washed up, Baldy."

Baldy? Michael repeated to himself.

"He is not washed up," Tweety peeped angrily.

"Shut up!" Pound swatted the bird across the room.

Quick as a flash, Michael scooped Tweety off the floor. "Are you okay?" he asked.

Tweety gazed up at Michael. "You're not scared of them, are you, Michael?"

Michael set Tweety down gently. He looked at all the Looney Tunes. Each one gazed back, hopeful.

Michael stood up tall. He threw back his shoulders and smiled. "Let's play some basketball!" he said.

12

The Looney Tune gym was buzzing. It was time for the Tune Squad drills.

"Has anyone ever played basketball?" Michael asked.

Only one person answered. "Um, I have," said a shy-sounding voice.

A pretty bunny stepped onto the court. Bugs Bunny's heart did a flip-flop of joy.

"What's her name?" Michael whispered to Bugs.

"I don't know," Bugs whispered back. "But I'd sure like to meet her."

"My name is Lola Bunny," the bunny told them sweetly.

"Lola?" asked Bugs.

"Yes?" Lola answered, giggling softly.

"You want to play a little one-on-one, Doll?"

Lola's eyes narrowed. She stopped giggling.

"On the court, Bugs," she barked.

Bugs grabbed the ball and dribbled. He whipped the ball around his back and through his legs. Then he jumped for the basket, twirling the ball on one finger. Everyone gasped. What style. What grace.

What a block!

Lola came out of nowhere. She batted the ball to the ground. Then she landed gently on her feet.

She shot a steely look at Bugs. "Don't ever call me 'Doll.' "

"Check," Bugs agreed.

Lola giggled softly again. "Hey," she said sweetly. "Nice playing with you."

Well, at least we have one good player,

Michael thought. *But what about everyone else?*

And what about his feet? Michael was still wearing golf shoes.

"Can anyone lend me sneakers?" he asked.

"Sneakers?" said Bugs. He lifted one bare paw. Daffy checked his webbed feet. Nobody wore shoes except Yosemite Sam — and those were cowboy boots.

"Somebody has to get my gear," Michael went on. "And don't forget my North Carolina shorts. They're lucky. I wore them under my Bulls uniform every game."

"Peeeeeww!" said the Looney Tunes.

"Hey!" Michael protested. "I washed them every time!"

13

That night, Bugs and Daffy burrowed to Michael's house. Along the way Bugs checked a map. Then he popped up to see the neighborhood. "You'd better follow me," he told Daffy.

"I always follow the bunny," Daffy muttered.

Bugs popped up again. "We're right in front of Michael's house!"

"I knew that!" Daffy snapped.

"Okay," Bugs said. He pointed left. "Let's go in this way."

"I say let's go in *that* way." Daffy pointed right.

Then he scooted quickly away from Bugs.

"He just never learns," Bugs said shrugging and going the other way.

A minute later Daffy lit a match. How close was he? *Very close,* Daffy thought. *To the doghouse!*

"G-r-r-r!"

Daffy stood face-to-face with the snarling Charles. The bulldog growled. *Whoosh!* The match blew out.

Bugs, meanwhile, popped up in the Jordans' hallway. He was in!

Knock! Knock! Someone rapped at the door. Bugs tiptoed over to answer it.

The door creaked open. "Twinkle, twinkle," said Daffy as stars circled his head. Then he collapsed.

"Come on!" Bugs said, annoyed. Daffy was always fooling around! "We've got to find Michael's basketball stuff."

Daffy stumbled to his feet. Then he and Bugs snuck upstairs. Where was Michael's trophy room? Quietly they opened a door. *Creak!* Inside her bedroom, Jasmine was fast asleep.

"You know," Daffy complained, peeking in, "I'm getting tired of all this running around."

Jasmine opened her eyes. After Bugs and Daffy left, she jumped out of bed. And when they finally reached the trophy room, Jasmine . . . and Marcus . . . and Jeffrey were right behind them.

Quickly Bugs and Daffy stuffed sneakers and T-shirts into a gym bag. They thought they had everything. But then they remembered.

"The shorts!" they both cried. Where were the lucky shorts?

Daffy opened a closet. "I found them!" he called. Then he saw Charles crouched inside, the shorts in his mouth. Daffy slammed the door shut.

A second later, the door crashed open. *Thump!* It fell onto Daffy. Daffy squeezed out and raced in back of Bugs.

"I'm right behind you, pal," he said bravely.

Charles padded forward, growling.

Bugs thought quickly. They needed those shorts! But they couldn't just grab them. So Bugs held a bone in front of Charles.

That should make him drop the shorts, Bugs thought. But no. Charles held on tight.

Next they tried a full-course dinner. They lowered it on a table, complete with candles and silverware. Still, Charles gripped the shorts tight.

From the doorway, Marcus whistled. Charles wagged his tail and headed over to the children.

"Give it to me, Charles," Jeffrey ordered. And he took the shorts from the bulldog's mouth.

"Here you go, Bugs," Jeff said, handing them over.

"Thanks, kid. Bye-bye."

"Hey! Where are you going?" Jeff asked.

"Don't tell anyone," Bugs said in a whisper, "but the Looney Tunes have a big basketball game and your dad's going to play!"

14

Vroom! Late that night, Stan drove across the golf course in a giant bulldozer.

I'll dig a huge crater by the golf hole, he thought. *I'll find Michael Jordan. Even if I have to dig forever!*

Stan wiped his brow. Something strange was happening. First there was the problem with the NBA players. They still couldn't catch or shoot or dribble. They fell and slid and fumbled the ball.

The players got X rays and laser beams. They talked about their feelings and their dreams. But nothing helped. Doctors didn't know what to do.

And what about Michael? Where was he?

"This is it, Mike!" Stan called.

Then he heard voices. *Strange,* he thought. *It sounds like Bugs Bunny and Daffy Duck.* He squinted into the dark.

It *was* Bugs and Daffy, coming up to check their map. And they had Michael's gym bag! They knew where he was!

Stan watched them disappear down another hole. So he sucked in his breath. And he followed them.

Minutes later, Stan stepped into the Looney Tune gym. Michael was warming up.

"Let's see if I remember how to play," Michael said. He dunked. He spun. He dribbled.

The Looney Tunes looked on, in awe.

Stan raced over and hugged Michael tight. "Is it really you?" he breathed.

All around them, cartoon characters

tried to be like Mike. They raced and dribbled and shot.

And missed.

This is no place for Michael Jordan, Stan thought.

"I'm taking you back," Stan told him. "You have baseball practice."

Michael shook his head. "I can't go. I'm helping my friends in a basketball game. And it's just about to start."

"Uh, Michael," Stan said in a low voice. "Do you know your friends are cartoon characters?"

"Yeah," Michael said a little angrily. "So?"

"Doesn't bother you?" Stan said backing off. "Then it doesn't bother me. Let me help," he pleaded suddenly. "I may not be very tall. But I am slow and large. I'll do anything, Michael. Anything!"

"Anything?" Michael asked.

"Anything!" Stan repeated.

Michael pointed to the bench. "Then sit right here."

15

The Looney Tune stadium was jam-packed. Fans roared. Everyone screamed. Swackhammer sat in the audience, grinning. *Those Looney Tunes don't have a chance,* he thought.

Then the starting players for the Tune Squad were introduced.

"Standing two feet four," the announcer cried, "The Wonder from Down Under!"

The Tasmanian Devil whirled onto the court. Everyone clapped.

"The Heartthrob of the Hoops," the

announcer called, "Lola Bunny!"

Lola loped out gracefully. The crowd went wild.

"The Quackster of the Court, Daffy Duck!"

Daffy's mom went wild.

"And at three feet two, not including ears — Bugs Bunny!"

Everyone whistled and stamped their feet.

"And now the player-coach. At six feet six. From North Carolina. His Royal Highness . . . Michaellllll Jorrrdannn!"

Wild screams rocked the stadium. *Whoosh!* Off blew the roof. When it settled back down, Michael called the team together.

"You guys ready?" Michael asked.

Daffy hopped up and down. "I'm set to take it to the rack, Jack."

"Those Monstars will wish they'd never been born," said Tweety, just as excited.

"We're going to steamroll them, Doc," Bugs added loudly. He jumped around and around in circles. "Hit and run!"

"Guys," Michael said. "Let's just go out and have fun."

The team cheered loudly — until the Monstars ran on court.

The aliens seemed bigger. Stronger. *Boom!* Pound dribbled a ball. *Boom!* The floor split in two. Bugs had to zip it together before the game could start.

Finally the teams got into place. Tiny Marvin the Martian tossed the ball for the jump. Then he sprang away from the Monstars' giant feet.

Up and up the players leaped. Michael soared above the others. He tapped the ball to Bugs.

"I got it!" Bugs shouted. "I got the ball."

But what should he do with it?

The Monstars charged. Pound plowed into Bugs, grabbing the ball. He hammered his way to the basket. Two points!

Michael called for time-out. "Are you all right?" he asked Bugs.

"Did we lose?" Bugs mumbled in a daze.

"It's two to nothing," Michael told him.

"Whew!" Bugs said. "Close game."

The buzzer sounded. The game started once again; Tune Squad's ball.

Michael dribbled across court. He raced around Bang and Blanko. He darted between Bupkus and Nawt. He spun past Pound, driving to the basket. He scored!

Two to two. Tie score.

The next thing Daffy knew, *he* had the ball. He held it tight. *Boom! Boom!* The Monstars pounded toward him. Closer. Closer. What could he do?

He threw the ball to Stan, sitting on the bench.

Marvin blew his whistle. Monstar ball. The Tunes turned to Daffy, glaring.

"He was wide open," Daffy explained.

Then Sylvester jumped into the game. But all he could think of was Tweety. He stuffed the bird into his mouth.

Suddenly the ball hit Sylvester in the stomach. *Foomph!* It knocked the breath — and Tweety — right out of him.

And the Monstars scooped up the ball.

Foghorn Leghorn took the ball out-of-bounds. He dribbled. Grinning, Nawt stomped over to guard him. He towered over Foghorn and roared. His breath came out in a fiery spurt.

"Did you order crispy chicken?" Foghorn asked, his feathers black and burned.

The Monstars nabbed the ball.

Then when Lola had the ball, Pound stepped up close. "Try to get by me, doll!" he jeered.

Lola's sweet gaze turned steely. In a flash, she spun past Pound. Then she hopped and slam-dunked over his head. Another two points for the Tunes.

"Don't ever call me 'doll,'" Lola said.

But the Monstars passed and blocked. They shot and dunked. They played hard — and tricky. Michael did his best. They all did. But the Monstars were too much.

The buzzer sounded for halftime. Michael eyed the scoreboard. Monstars: 64, Tune Squad: 18.

16

Michael and the Tune Squad trailed into the locker room.

Sylvester sighed. "Moron Mountain, here we come."

"Come on, guys," Michael said brightly. "We have a whole second half to play."

"Zippity doo daa," Daffy mumbled. He rubbed his sore webbed feet. "I can't wait."

Stan saw the long faces. He couldn't let this happen — not to Michael's new friends. He snuck inside the Monstars' locker room.

Inside, Swackhammer was giving a pep talk. "Not bad for the first half," he said in a nasty voice. "But we've got to keep it up."

"No problem," bellowed Pound. "Remember? We stole our power from the NBA!"

"Shut up!" ordered Swackhammer. He sniffed the air. "I smell something."

Blanko sniffed his armpit.

"Not you, you idiot!" cried Swackhammer. He followed his nose to a locker. He flung open the door. Stan cowered inside.

"A spy!" sneered Swackhammer. He signaled the others. And they all closed in.

"We've got to come together," Michael was saying in the other locker room. "We can still win this thing. We've got to believe in ourselves."

Just then Stan stumbled in. His glasses were lopsided. His hair stood on end.

"Gwacious!" said Elmer Fudd.

"The Monstars!" gasped Stan. "They

stole their power from Charles Barkley, Patrick Ewing, and the other NBA stars!"

"So that's what happened," Michael said slowly.

The members of the Tune Squad hung their heads even lower. No way could they win. They were up against the best in the world.

"I think we should qui-qui-qui — f-f-for-feit!" stuttered Porky.

"Yeah!" the others echoed.

Everyone wanted to give up? Michael couldn't believe it! What happened to team spirit? And believing in yourself?

"Listen up!" Michael demanded. His voice grew louder and louder. He wanted everyone to feel his excitement. "I wasn't dragged down here to lose. We're letting those Monstars push us around. And I'm not going out like that! We've got to fight back. We've got to get right in their faces. What do you say?"

There wasn't any answer. Everyone had fallen asleep.

"Great speech and all, Doc," Bugs told Michael. "But didn't you forget something? Your secret stuff?"

Secret stuff? Everyone blinked awake. What secret stuff?

Bugs winked at Michael. Then he held out a bottle of water. He took a sip. All at once, his muscles bulged. His ears stood up straight. He was bigger. Stronger.

Sylvester reached for the bottle. "Have you been holding out?" he asked Michael.

"No," Michael said, thinking quickly. "I didn't think you needed it. You're all so tough!"

Foghorn Leghorn took a chug. "We're also chicken," he said.

Each character drank deeply, then passed the water on. Their eyes grew bright. They stood up tall, ready to play.

"Now, let's go out there!" Michael yelled.

As the Tunes broke into a cheer, Daffy tossed the bottle into the air. Stan caught it awkwardly. And he drank the very last drop.

17

The second half began with a bang. Michael was all over the court. Stealing. Shooting. Rebounding. And the Looney Tunes were right behind him.

Wile E. Coyote blew up the Monstar basket with dynamite.

Pepe Le Pew scampered onto the court. He held up his little skunk tail.

"Pew!" cried the Monstars, fainting. Pepe grabbed the ball and scored.

The Tune Squad was gaining fast.

Monstars: 66, Tune Squad: 28
Monstars: 68, Tune Squad: 41
Monstars: 70, Tune Squad: 66

"Bombs away!" shouted Tweety.

"Time out!" screamed Swackhammer. "Why didn't you get this guy Jordan?" he howled at the aliens.

"He quit the NBA," said Pound.

"He's a baseball player," Bupkus added.

"Yeah, boss, a baseball player," Nawt echoed.

"Well, *he's* the one I want for Moron Mountain," Swackhammer yelled.

Michael turned to Swackhammer, over-hearing. He'd just had a great idea.

"Hey!" he yelled back. "How about this? If we win, you give the NBA players their talent back. If you win, you get me!"

Swackhammer nodded slowly. "You'll be our star attraction. You'll sign auto-graphs. You'll play one-on-one with the customers. And lose."

Michael shook Swackhammer's hand.

"Deal!" Then he turned to his teammates. They all looked worried. "I have faith in you," Michael told them.

Swackhammer faced the Monstars. "Crush 'em," he growled.

Time-out was over. Once again, Michael had the ball. And Blanko wanted it. He aimed a flying tackle. But Michael sidestepped him. *Thwack!* Blanko knocked Daffy over instead.

Daffy flew back . . . and back . . . and up into the stands. For a moment he disappeared from view. Then he shot up through a popcorn box — just in time to see Michael hit a big three-pointer.

Pound growled. He looked over at his teammates and nodded. It was time for some down-and-dirty playing.

Pound climbed up the backboard. He spread his arms and dove, aiming right for Lola. *Zzzip!* Bugs raced over and pushed her out of the way. *Crash!* Bugs went down instead.

And the Monstars kept coming. They side-armed the Tune Squad players. They clipped them. And tricked them. And pushed and tripped and cheated them.

The Tune Squad grew more and more determined. They wouldn't—they couldn't!—let the Monstars win. But the Squad was in terrible shape. Michael's eyes swept the bench. His friends were bandaged and stitched. They held crutches under their arms and ice packs to their knees.

Michael needed another player. But only one person could step in. Only one person could stand.

Stan.

18

"You're in, Stan," Michael ordered.

Stan leaped to his feet. This was his chance. His moment. He trotted onto the basketball court. Eyes darting, he took in the action.

Oh! he realized. *I'm all alone, right near the basket.*

"Michael!" he shouted. "I'm open! I'm open!"

Monstars surrounded Michael. Desperate, he tossed the ball to Stan. Stan closed his eyes. The ball dropped into his hands. Quick as a flash, the Monstars piled on top.

Stan squirmed at the bottom of the heap. He wriggled one arm free. Then he tossed the ball without looking.

The ball curved in the air. Slowly it dropped. Lower. Lower. *Swish!* Into the basket.

Monstars: 89, Tune Squad: 88

Time left: 10 seconds

One by one, the Monstars jumped to their feet. But Stan stayed on the ground, flattened into a pancake.

Michael dashed over to help. "Stan!" he cried.

A second later, Foghorn whipped out a stretcher. He scraped Stan off the floor and flipped him onto a stretcher like an over easy egg. *Pop!* Stan inflated to his old round shape.

Michael gazed at him, amazed. *How did he do that?*

"This is Looney Tune Land," Bugs explained. He stretched his arm out long as a snake. "Anybody can do it."

Michael grinned as Stan was carried out. He'd grown kind of fond of the chubby little guy. He hated to see him hurt. But Stan was going to be just fine. So there was only one problem left. Michael still needed another player.

And Daffy needed more of that secret stuff.

"But it was just water," Michael told him. "You guys had the special stuff inside you all along."

Daffy's eyes opened wide. That meant the Tune Squad was a pretty good team. They could really win. But what about a fifth player? If they didn't find one, they would forfeit the game.

"Forfeit?" Michael repeated, disappointed. He shook his head, trying to think of another way. Another answer. But there was none.

We've come so far, he thought. *Do we have to give up now?*

Just then the stadium doors blew open. A strong wind swept across the court. Twigs and tumbleweed flew all around.

Michael shielded his eyes against the wind. There was something in the distance . . . something coming closer . . . and closer. . . . Could it be? Yes!

"Beep beep!"

It was the Road Runner.

The Road Runner jumped into the Tune Squad huddle. Michael clapped his hands.

"Listen," he told his teammates, "we've only got ten seconds. The Monstars have the ball. We have to go for the steal."

The buzzer sounded. And it all came down to one play.

19

Bupkus stood off court with the ball. He passed it to Pound.

Pound grinned nastily. He dribbled the ball. Once. Twice. Three times. He moved slowly, as if he was in no hurry at all. As if this game didn't matter in the least.

Michael clenched his teeth. He knew this plan. The Monstars were trying to run out the clock.

Seven seconds left.

Bugs lunged for the ball. He missed.

Six seconds left.

Daffy tap-danced around Pound. He grabbed for the ball. He almost had it . . . almost had it . . . but Pound scooted away.

Five seconds left.

"Beep! Beep!" Road Runner sped across the court.

Four seconds left.

He zipped around Pound so fast, Pound didn't see a thing.

And Road Runner had the ball!

He tossed it over to Michael. Michael snagged it.

Three seconds left.

Michael eyed the basket! Was it too far away?

Not in Looney Tune Land, he hoped.

Michael sprang into the air. And he stayed there. He was flying! Closer to the basket. And closer.

The Monstars lunged to stop him. Giant arms and legs wheeled all around. Michael swerved past them, flying higher and higher.

Two seconds left.

The Monstars leaped. They grabbed Michael's legs! They were holding him down. How could he make the basket now?

Michael stretched his body like a rubber band. Farther. Farther. Just like a cartoon!

One second left.

Michael brought his arms up high. Then he dropped them over the basket. *Boom!* A slam dunk, right at the buzzer!

Game over! The Tune Squad won by a point!

20

"Noooo!" screamed Swackhammer.

Cheers and shouts rang through the gym. The Tune Squad was free! No Moron Mountain! No prisoners!

Michael grinned at his Tune Squad friends. "Great skills!" he told the Road Runner. "Too bad you can't play in the NBA."

"Beep! Beep!" the Road Runner answered.

Meanwhile Pound trudged over to Swackhammer. "Sorry, boss," he said.

"We cheated as best we could."

Swackhammer turned an angry shade of purple. "Wait until I get you home," he hissed.

Michael stepped up to the giant aliens. "Why does he talk to you like that?" he asked. "Why do you let him?"

"Because he's bigger!" Nawt cried.

Slowly Pound smiled. He gazed over at Swackhammer . . . way over his head. He *used* to be bigger! Then all the aliens grinned. They understood, too! They gathered around Swackhammer. He backed away, frightened. But there was nowhere to go.

The Monstars tied him to a rocket. And he zoomed into space.

The Tune Squad cheered wildly and Michael grinned.

"Now, one more thing," Michael told the Monstars. "You've got to give my NBA pals their talent back."

The aliens nodded. It was part of the deal. They each touched the basketball.

The ball began to glow brighter and brighter just like before. And bit by bit, the aliens shrank and shrank. The power left their muscles like air from a balloon. The evil grins faded.

They were tiny Nerdlucks once again!

"Mr. Bunny?" Pound asked in his little squeaky voice. "Can we stay here? With you?"

The Nerdlucks made funny faces. They sang and danced and acted looney. *Not quite looney enough*, Bugs thought. *But maybe with some work . . .*

21

Michael packed the glowing basketball into his gym bag. It was time to go. He had a baseball game to play.

"I really enjoyed playing here," he told the Tune Squad. "You've got a lot . . . a lot . . ."

He couldn't think of the words. "Well," he finished, "you've got a lot of IT. Whatever *it* is."

The Tune Squad members shook Michael's hand again and again. After all,

Michael had shown them they could do anything. And Michael would miss them, too, that was for sure.

Then Michael and Stan jumped into the spaceship. They rocketed up, up, up to the real world.

Once again, the minor league stadium was packed. It was the last inning. The score was tied. And there were two outs. Michael's team needed him. Badly.

The crowd chanted, "We want Michael! We want Michael!"

But no one knew where he was.

"He's not back from his other game," Jeffrey said to Juanita.

"What game?" asked Juanita. But Jeffrey didn't answer. A shout rose from the stands. A spaceship hovered over the stadium!

Stan hurried down the ramp. "Ladies and gentlemen," he announced. "Michael Jordan!"

One basketball game down. One baseball game, too. Michael had led two teams to victory. But he still had one thing left to do. He had to help his NBA friends.

A little while later, he found them sitting in front of a basketball hoop. That's it. Just sitting.

"Want your games back?" he asked them.

Charles and the others looked at Michael. Was he crazy? Of course they did!

Michael showed them the glowing basketball. "Then touch this," he told them.

They all drew back. "You're crazy!" said Charles.

"No way!" said Muggsy.

"Not a chance!" said Patrick.

Michael went to put the ball in his bag. "Okay! So don't play basketball — ever!"

What did they have to lose? Shrugging, the players reached for the ball. They touched it.

Suddenly they twitched. They shook and danced and then they stopped.

Michael tossed Charles the ball. And Charles caught it! Then Charles bounced the ball to Patrick, and Patrick drove to the hoop.

"We're back!" cried Larry Johnson.

"Hey, Michael!" Charles said as they dribbled and dunked and shot. "Want to play?"

Patrick answered for him. "He doesn't play basketball anymore. Remember?"

Shawn Bradley grinned. "Maybe he just doesn't have it anymore."

Michael thought about the Tune Squad. About Bugs and Daffy and the way they played the game. Suddenly he made a decision.

"There's only one way to find out!" he said.

Michael Jordan — basketball legend — was back in the game!